To
The students at Hazlewood Elementary

THE WITCHES' LITTLE SISTER

JoAnne Nelson

Story by JoAnne Nelson
Illustrations by Jack McLellan

October, 2010

This book is dedicated to
my sister Kathy Frederick,
"the witches' little sister,"
and
to my granddaughter,
Courtney Nelson,
whose birthday is June 25th.

Published by SuperBooks, superbooks@superbooks.net
P.O. Box 1233, Edmonds WA 98020, phone: 800-278-8362 or 425-778-8362

Printed in China

ISBN -10: 1-881478-02-5
ISBN -13: 978-1-881478-02-7

Somewhere in the forest
in a spot so strange and rare
is a cozy little witches' house
with witches living there.

They have a little sister
who wants to learn to fly.
She has a magic witches' broom
and she really wants to try.

Jock McLellan
4/06 ©

So the witches had a meeting
on the 25th of June,
and decided they'd go riding
in and out around the moon.

They gathered all together
in the corner of the room.
But the witches' little sister
forgot to bring her broom.

JUNE
25

They sent her off to get it,
and she brought it to the room.
It was frazzled and bedraggled,
an unbewitching sort of broom.

They didn't think she'd make it
going up there to the moon.
But the little witch insisted
she'd be with them very soon.

Then they started to get ready.
They put all their gear in stacks.
They had broomsticks, cats and lanterns
and just ordinary packs.

SECURITY >
POTION
RUSH
TOILET PAPER
SPARE
HAIR DRYER
UPS
UPS
FRAGIL

When they got it all together,
they sat down to have a chat.
But the witches' little sister
forgot to bring her hat.

They sent her off to get it,
she looked puzzled and she frowned
Wherever had she put it?
She looked outside on the ground.

She looked upstairs in the closet.
She looked underneath the mat.
And finally she found it.
She found her witches' hat.

When they trooped out
to the launch pad
at the edge of Shadow Lake
the little witch remembered
a fact that made her shake.

They were almost set for take-off.
The lake was calm and flat.
When the witches' little sister
ran back to get her cat.

She looked upstairs and downstairs.
She looked underneath her bed.
Then she finally remembered
it was hiding in the shed.

When she put it in the wagon
it looked a little fat.
But the witches' little sister
just had to bring her cat.

BAGGAGE
CHECK - IN

Out there at the launch pad
The witches were in line.
The broomsticks were all ready,
and the cats were doing fine.

Oh, the witches they were ready
to take off into the night.
But the witches' little sister
forgot to bring her light.

She hurried to the workshop
which was somewhere in the back.
She grabbed the nearest lantern
and put it in her pack.

Her hat was tipping slightly,
as she held on to the light.
Then she rode off on her broomstick
into the starry night.

The cat stirred only slightly
while it slept upon her bed.
But it woke her from her dream enough,
just to clear her sleepy head.

She wasn't flying through the stars
on her magic witches' broom.
She was right there in her little bed
in her warm and cozy room.

SWEET DREAMS

TO LAUNCH
PAD